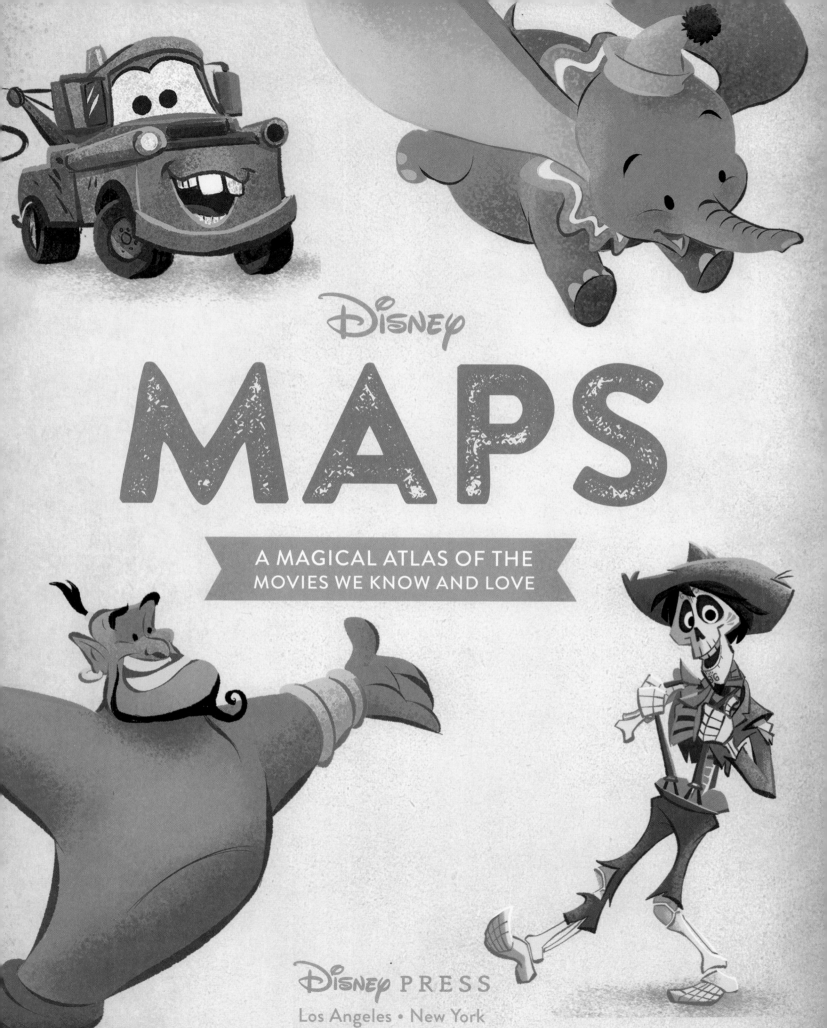

Disney
MAPS

A MAGICAL ATLAS OF THE
MOVIES WE KNOW AND LOVE

Disney PRESS

Los Angeles • New York

FOREWORD

When it comes to letting your eyes roam and explore, who doesn't love a map? Maps can make you feel like you're practically there. Sometimes a map is even better than the real thing; you walk around a place in your mind, picking out exactly what you want to see.

Ancient mapmakers were out to capture attention. They lavished gold leaf and ornate ornamental designs on their work, knowing their maps would be scrutinized by many for more than just information. And though they're largely unnecessary in today's technological world, we still use maps to adorn our homes and public spaces.

Before they were drawn or intricately charted, the very first maps were likely inside people's minds. The seafaring people of Polynesia were able to navigate the entire Pacific Ocean with only a mental image and some help from the stars. Polynesians who met explorer James Cook and naturalist Joseph Banks in the 1700s were baffled by their paper maps. Why would anyone need to write down the location of hundreds of islands when you can see those locations in your mind? Given our ability to do this, it makes sense that maps connect us to a rich inner world, to places we've been before, in real life or in our imaginations.

In this book, you'll see maps of places that never really existed. The sets for the films were, of course, created by many talented and imaginative people, but it may surprise you to find they were also shaped by the stories they service. Since I can't speak to the specific experiences of all the filmmakers reflected in this book, I'll give you a few examples from the films I worked on to explain how the sets and environments were affected in unexpected ways by the stories and characters.

Locations in movies are crucial to the storytelling. This is because the locations themselves have significant meaning and reflect the main character's internal change. In *Up*, we placed Paradise Falls at one end of a mountaintop and our beloved giant bird Kevin's home on the other end. We literally mapped out Carl Fredricksen's journey, knowing it would present him with a tough choice about where to go. Movement toward Paradise Falls at screen right indicated Carl's desire to stay

disconnected and detached from the world, and moving toward screen left meant he was starting to care about Russell, Dug, and Kevin. If we placed the waterfalls and the bird's home next to each other, Carl could just take the bird home on his way to the falls, and we wouldn't have a story.

It surprises most people to learn that our environments do not come into complete focus until the film is finished. Much like the characters on-screen, the set mutates and moves around as the story grows. *Inside Out* was a story about Joy returning to Headquarters, an isolated office in the center of Riley's mind. But until Joy learned to trust Sadness and move past Riley's childhood—represented by her imaginary friend, Bing Bong—we couldn't let her return. The locations in our story were proving grounds for Joy's growth. As our story developed, we understood more and more about what Joy needed to learn, so several sets were redesigned and relocated more than once to allow for Joy's emotional development. This is how Joy, Sadness, and Bing Bong ended up taking that perilous shortcut through Abstract Thought, missing the Train of Thought, and waiting at Imagination Land for the next pickup.

Then, too, as in real life, locations become reflections of the people who inhabit those spaces. Carl and Ellie's home in *Up*—from its intimate, memory-filled rooms to its bright, colorful exterior walls—reflects their life together, and almost on its own, tells their story. Our outer spaces give the world a peek into our inner self; how we think and see ourselves—or, perhaps, how we'd like to been seen by others.

When you walk through the beautiful maps in this book, you'll go on a journey, not only inside your own mind, but into the stories of your favorite characters. Enjoy the ride!

PETE DOCTER

Director, *Monsters, Inc.*; *Up*; *Inside Out*
Chief Creative Officer, Pixar Animation Studios

SNOW WHITE AND THE SEVEN DWARFS
1937

PINOCCHIO
1940

DUMBO
1941

ALICE IN WONDERLAND
1951

PETER PAN
1953

ONE HUNDRED AND ONE DALMATIANS
1961

THE JUNGLE BOOK
1967

THE LITTLE MERMAID
1989

BEAUTY AND THE BEAST
1991

ALADDIN
1992

THE LION KING
1994

TOY STORY
1995

A BUG'S LIFE
1998

FINDING NEMO
2003

THE INCREDIBLES
2004

CARS
2006

RATATOUILLE
2007

UP
2009

BRAVE
2012

MONSTERS UNIVERSITY
2013

FROZEN
2013

INSIDE OUT
2015

MOANA
2016

COCO
2017

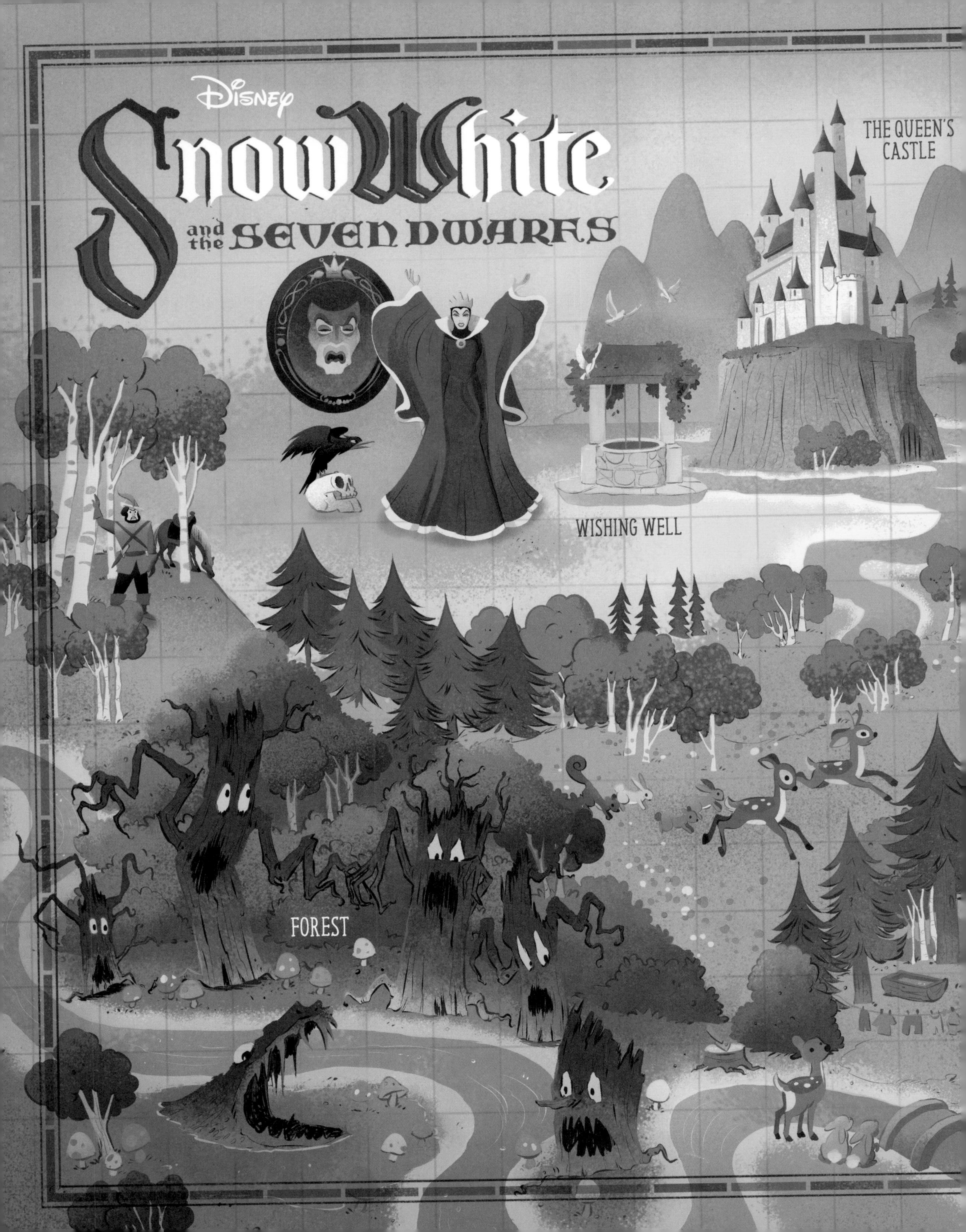

DISNEY

Snow White
and the SEVEN DWARFS

THE QUEEN'S CASTLE

WISHING WELL

FOREST

THE PRINCE'S CASTLE

MINE

DWARFS'
MINE

COTTAGE OF THE
SEVEN DWARFS

Disney
Snow White
and the SEVEN DWARFS

Snow White's kingdom is a place where one can get swept away in darkness and fear before being restored by kindness and the strength of love. It ranges from the idyllic to the terrifying, depending on where you look.

In one glance, you see a magnificent castle stretching above a vast kingdom, but up in a window an evil ruling queen casts a dark gaze across the land. You may hear a sweet voice singing wishes into a well, but then see a young princess forced into rags by her jealous stepmother. A grand forest beckons to a lover of nature, home to sweet woodland creatures and wildflowers, but it's also home to gnarled, twisted trees and dark shadows hiding possible danger.

Luckily for Snow White, these woods are also a place where kind dwarfs toil in a mine, harvesting beautiful gems, living peacefully in a modest cottage, and offering refuge to a stranger who happens upon their door.

MOMENTS TO REMEMBER

- After the Queen is told by her magic mirror that Snow White is the "fairest of them all," she orders the Hunstman to take the girl to the forest and kill her. Unable to do the deed, the Huntsman urges Snow White to run away.

- The Dwarfs return home from working in the mine and see that someone has been in their cottage. Fearing it to be a ghost, a goblin, a thief, or a dragon, they make their way slowly upstairs and discover Snow White.

- The Queen descends to her evil dungeon lair, using her magic to make a poison apple and transform into a wretched old hag in an effort to fool Snow White and get rid of her for good.

- When Snow White falls victim to the Queen's sleeping curse, the Dwarfs place her in a coffin made of glass and gold. The Prince comes to give Snow White Love's First Kiss, lifting the curse.

STEPS TO CLEAN THE DWARFS' COTTAGE

- Deer, bunnies, and squirrels use their tails to dust.

- Turtles help clear the stacks of cups and plates.

- Squirrels, chipmunks, fawns, and bluebirds wash and dry dirty dishes.

- Squirrels and chipmunks clear cobwebs.

- Birds pick and arrange fresh flowers from the forest.

- Raccoons and turtles work together to launder clothes.

- Birds wring out and hang clothes to dry.

- Snow White takes care of the sweeping while chipmunks hold the dustpan.

All of the above is done with a song.

CHARACTERS

SNOW WHITE

THE QUEEN

GRUMPY

DOPEY

DOC

SNEEZY

HAPPY

BASHFUL

SLEEPY

THE PRINCE

THE MAGIC MIRROR

THE HUNTSMAN

THE WITCH

Disney
Pinocchio
Red Lobster Inn
THE RED LOBSTER INN
GEPPETTO'S
WORKSHOP
N
W
E
S
MONSTRO THE WHALE

THE DOCKS

PLEASURE
ISLAND

STROMBOLI'S
CART

Pinocchio

Pinocchio's village, "pretty as a picture" in Jiminy Cricket's words, is a quaint, sleepy town with magic lurking in its seams. It's a place where good, innocent people live their lives and dream their dreams alongside seedier characters who scheme their schemes and con their cons.

Geppetto seems content with his simple life, toiling away in his wood-carving workshop with his pets to keep him company. Then, one day, he's delightfully surprised to find that his wooden puppet boy has been brought to life by a fairy. After celebrating, his first order of business is to send his new son to school like all the other children. Pinocchio, however, unaccustomed to the world, never makes it to school.

He's drawn to flashier trappings in the village, from con men to a traveling marionette show to the cursed Pleasure Island. When Pinocchio finally realizes the error of his ways, it takes a trip to the bottom of the ocean and into the belly of a beast to redeem himself and become a real boy.

MOMENTS TO REMEMBER

- Have you ever wished upon a star? Geppetto has! His wish upon a star summons the Blue Fairy into his workshop, where she casts her magic to bring a wooden puppet named Pinocchio to life.

- When the Blue Fairy finds Pinocchio trapped in Stromboli's cart, he lies to her about his reasons for avoiding school, causing his nose to grow so long it sprouts leaves!

- The boys brought to Pleasure Island suffer a terrifying fate: they're transformed into donkeys! Luckily, Pinocchio escapes before he's fully changed.

- Trapped in the belly of an enormous whale, Pinocchio comes up with a clever plan for escape. He and Geppetto build a fire in hopes the smoke will cause the creature to sneeze the family out— and it works!

THINGS FOUND IN GEPPETTO'S WORKSHOP

- Intricately carved clocks

- Jars of paint

- Music boxes

- Shelves of wooden and stuffed toys

- Puppets

- Hanging birdcages

- Piggy banks

- Figurines

- Musical instruments

- Firewood and fireplace

- Plenty of candles

- Wood shavings

CHARACTERS

PINOCCHIO

GEPPETTO

THE BLUE FAIRY

JIMINY CRICKET

LAMPWICK

STROMBOLI

HONEST JOHN

GIDEON

THE COACHMAN

CLEO

FIGARO

MONSTRO

Disney
DUMBO
GEORGIA
61
STORE
ALABAMA
MISSISSIPPI
GULF COAST
N
E
W
S

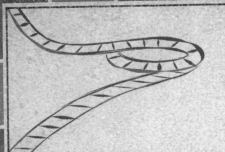

Disney
DUMBO

Circuses are filled with extraordinary sights and amazing feats. The circus has been Dumbo the elephant's home ever since he was dropped off as a baby by Mr. Stork, but it takes him a while to truly fit in. As he grows up, his circus home travels across the country from its winter quarters in Florida. The living, breathing, and sometimes sleeping train, Casey Jr., takes the circus and its tents, performers, workers, and animals everywhere they need to go.

Whenever Casey Jr. reaches a destination, the circus workers and elephants unpack the train and work all night to set up tents for sleeping as well as for performing. Crowds flock to the big top but stop at sideshows along the way. One of these sideshows is the menagerie, where exotic animals are put on display, including Dumbo and his mother, Mrs. Jumbo. When Dumbo does get the chance to perform in the big top, it doesn't go so well—that is, until Dumbo pulls off an all-star act of his very own.

MOMENTS TO REMEMBER

- Dumbo is actually a nickname! The baby elephant's real name is Jumbo Jr.

- Dumbo makes his very first friend when Timothy Q. Mouse finds him getting picked on by the other elephants. Timothy takes the young elephant under his wing and vows to help him.

- After Dumbo makes an elephant-sized mistake during his first act, he's forced to become a clown, dress up like a baby, and jump from a tower so the clown "firemen" can save him.

- Timothy realizes that Dumbo's ears may be good for something other than tripping up the little elephant. He gets the idea that Dumbo could use his ears as wings. With a great leap and a lot of courage, Dumbo soon finds himself really flying!

CIRCUS ATTRACTIONS

- Menagerie

- Various sideshows

- Clowns

- Marching band

- Parade

- Pyramid of pachyderms

- Flying elephant!

CHARACTERS

DUMBO　　　TIMOTHY Q. MOUSE　　　MRS. JUMBO　　　CASEY JR.

MR. STORK　　　THE RINGMASTER　　　GOSSIPING ELEPHANTS　　　TIGER

KANGAROOS　　　GIRAFFES

Disney

ALICE in WONDERLAND

DOWN THE RABBIT HOLE

MEADOW OF LIVING FLOWERS

POOL OF TEARS

WHITE RABBIT'S COTTAGE

Disney
ALICE
in
WONDERLAND

As long as you're imaginatively curious (or is it curiously imaginative?), you can make your way through the silly, serious, illogical, logical, colorful, mysterious world of Wonderland. Alice finds her way there by gently floating down a rabbit hole and then washing through a keyhole on a flood of her own tears. There are likely other methods of entry (through a looking glass is one).

However you get there, you will not be disappointed in the variety of places to explore and marvels to behold. And once you think you've seen it all, simply take a potion and shrink down to the size of an insect for an altogether different perspective—or if you'd rather, take a bite of a mushroom and grow taller than the trees for a bird's-eye view.

From ocean to forest, from royal maze to singing flower garden, there's truly something for everyone in Wonderland.

MOMENTS TO REMEMBER

- During Alice's descent down the rabbit hole, she passes many objects such as a lamp, a book, a mirror, and even a rocking chair where she briefly relaxes.

- Alice is delighted to find a cat perched in a tree. But with his tendency to fade in and out of visibility, remove his head to stand on it, and give confusing directions, the Cheshire Cat doesn't prove much help.

- Alice joins the Mad Hatter and the March Hare for a very different kind of tea party. In Wonderland, unbirthdays (the 364 days a year it is not one's birthday) are celebrated with tea and cake.

- Alice, having angered the Queen of Hearts, faces trial with witnesses and an audience consisting of characters she's met through her adventure. Luckily, she manages to escape, going back through the maze, tea party, caucus race, and more!

WONDERLAND KEY FACTS

- GOVERNMENT: Monarchy

- LANGUAGES SPOKEN: English; Nonsense

- BIRD: For croquet, the queen favors flamingos.

- FLOWER: Red rose

CHARACTERS

ALICE

THE WHITE RABBIT

THE CHESHIRE CAT

THE CATERPILLAR

THE QUEEN OF HEARTS

THE KING OF HEARTS

THE MAD HATTER

THE MARCH HARE

TWEEDLEDEE AND TWEEDLEDUM

THE WALRUS AND THE CARPENTER

CARD SOLDIERS

THE DOORKNOB

FLOWERS

THE DODO

DINAH

BUD

Disney
Peter Pan
MISTY MOUNTAINS
NATIVE CAMP
CANNIBAL COV
JOLLY ROGER

SKULL ROCK

MERMAID LAGOON

BLIND MAN'S BLUFF

PEG LEG
POINT

Disney
Peter Pan

With a pinch of pixie dust, a lot of imagination, and perhaps a bit of help from Peter Pan himself, the way to Never Land is simple: find the second star to the right, then go straight on till morning. Never Land is a lush island filled with pirates, Lost Boys, Natives, mermaids, many different species of wild animals, pixies, and one very hungry, ticking crocodile.

Never Land dominates the stories and playtime in the London nursery of Wendy, John, and Michael Darling, much to their father's dismay. The island promises adventure for anyone who visits, and it has the unique characteristic of ensuring its inhabitants will never grow up. For the Darlings, a trip there is, quite literally, a dream come true!

MOMENTS TO REMEMBER

- Peter Pan flies into the Darling nursery in search of the shadow he left behind. Wendy helps Peter sew his shadow back on, and in return, Peter teaches Wendy, John, and Michael how to fly, taking them on a trip through the skies of London to his home, Never Land.

- Peter rescues Tiger Lily from Skull Rock by using its unique cavernous geography to throw his voice and trick Captain Hook and Mr. Smee.

- Captain Hook tricks Tinker Bell into revealing the location of Peter Pan's hideout. The pirates capture Wendy, her brothers, and the Lost Boys and take them back to the *Jolly Roger*. All looks lost until Peter Pan arrives to save the day!

- It's not just humans who can fly with the help of pixie dust . . . the *Jolly Roger* sails into the sky, leaving Never Land and taking the Darling children home through an ocean of stars.

FOLLOWING THE LEADER FINDS

- Waterfall
- Stepping-stones
- Hippos
- Climbing vines
- Monkeys
- Grassy fields
- Rhinos
- Bears
- Mysterious footprints

CHARACTERS

PETER PAN

TINKER BELL

CAPTAIN HOOK

MR. SMEE

WENDY DARLING

JOHN DARLING

MICHAEL DARLING

NANA

THE CHIEF

TIGER LILY

THE CROCODILE

THE LOST BOYS

MERMAIDS

Disney

101 DALMATIANS

COLONEL'S HOUSE

DINSFORD

CRUELLA DE VIL'S HOUSE

HELL HALL

REGENT'S PARK

RADCLIFFES' RESIDENCE

Disney
101 DALMATIANS

Pongo and Perdita are perfectly content in their London townhome in the hustle and bustle of a neighborhood near Regent's Park. But when their puppies are kidnapped by Cruella De Vil, they have to tap into a regional network of information only animals can access—the Twilight Bark. Atop Primrose Hill in the park, Pongo and Perdita bark out to animals across the city in search of news about their missing pups.

Word comes back all the way from the countryside that their babies are being held in a decrepit old manor, Hell Hall. Pongo and Perdita set off on an epic adventure through city, suburb, and farmland to find their puppies, and nothing holds them back—not even the snowy winter weather and an icy river crossing.

MOMENTS TO REMEMBER

- When Pongo spots Anita and Perdita through a window, he leads Roger to Regent's Park so they can all meet.

- Pongo and Perdita become parents to fifteen puppies. When Anita's old classmate Cruella De Vil stops by the townhome, she takes an immediate interest in the puppies.

- Horace and Jasper steal the puppies and take them to Hell Hall, where eighty-four other Dalmatian puppies are also being held.

- Patch and Lucky's tumble into the fireplace gives Pongo the idea to cover all the dogs in soot, disguising them as Labradors to sneak past Cruella.

- When the dogs arrive back at Roger and Anita's townhome, the couple is overjoyed to be reunited with their pets. They decide they'll keep the other puppies, too, and purchase a country home: a Dalmatian Plantation!

PATH OF THE TWILIGHT BARK

- Pongo and Perdita, Primrose Hill

- Great Dane and terrier, Hampstead

- Scottish terrier and Afghan hound, London home

- Miscellaneous puppies and bulldog, London pet shop

- Poodle and other dogs, streets of London

- Dog, farmhouse

- Dog, barge

- Towser and Lucy, Suffolk County

- The Captain, Sergeant Tibs, and the Colonel, stables at the Colonel's house in Suffolk county

CHARACTERS

 ROGER

 ANITA

 PONGO

 PERDITA

 CRUELLA DE VIL

 HORACE

 JASPER

 NANNY

 THUNDERBOLT

 PATCH

 PENNY

 LUCKY

 ROLLY

 THE COLONEL

 SERGEANT TIBS

 THE CAPTAIN

 TOWSER

 LUCY

Disney

THE JUNGLE BOOK

VULTURE LANDING

KAA'S TREE

COUNCIL ROCK

WOLF DEN

ANCIENT
RUINS

MAN-VILLAGE

DISNEY
THE JUNGLE BOOK

The wild forests of India are not a safe place for a human to roam—unless that human was raised among the animals as one of their own. For in the world of the jungle, rules are different, dangers are different, food is different, life is different. The love of family, however, remains the same—something worth fighting for.

We see the jungle through Mowgli's adventures as he's reluctantly ushered from the family of wolves he's known since infancy to the foreign and strange human village.

The landscape of the jungle is green and fertile with both rough and gentle terrain: plains where elephants can patrol, rocky outcroppings where wolf pups can duck for safety, tall trees where snakes can stretch and lurk, lazy rivers where lazy bears can float, ancient ruins where monkeys can rule, and dying lands where vultures can roost comfortably. Mowgli makes it through alive, but not without a few close calls and the help of some very good friends.

MOMENTS TO REMEMBER

- When Mowgli is ten years old, the tiger, Shere Khan, returns to his part of the jungle. The wolf elders meet at Council Rock and decide that for everyone's safety, Mowgli must be sent to the Man-village.

- On his way through the jungle to the village with Bagheera the panther, Mowgli encounters the bear Baloo. Mowgli is drawn to Baloo's easygoing lifestyle.

- A group of monkeys kidnap Mowgli and take him to the ruins where an orangutan, King Louie, resides. Luckily, Baloo and Bagheera help Mowgli escape.

- With the help of the vultures, Mowgli and Baloo defeat Shere Khan. Baloo and Bagheera escort Mowgli out of the jungle and into the village, where he can live safely.

JUNGLE FRIENDS OF MOWGLI

- Wolf pack
- Bagheera
- Baloo
- Dawn Patrol elephants
- Vultures

JUNGLE ENEMIES OF MOWGLI

- King Louie and the monkeys
- Kaa
- Shere Khan

CHARACTERS

MOWGLI   BALOO   BAGHEERA   KAA

SHERE KHAN   KING LOUIE   RAMA   THE GIRL

COLONEL HATHI   THE BABY ELEPHANT   THE VULTURES

Disney

THE LITTLE MERMAID

PRINCE ERIC'S SHIP

KING TRITON'S PALACE

ARIEL'S GROTTO

PRINCE ERIC'S CASTLE

URSULA'S
LAIR

THE LAGOON

DISNEY
THE LITTLE
MERMAID

The proper place for a mermaid, you would think, is under the sea. Atlantica is an immense undersea kingdom filled with fish, crustaceans, mermaids, sunken ships, a castle, and an ambitious sea witch. As incredible as this world may be, though, it's the world above land that inspires the mermaid princess Ariel.

Prince Eric's kingdom is full of things that are ordinary to us but marvelous to Ariel, from bathtubs to clothes to silverware. Lucky enough to visit the prince's seaside castle, Ariel discovers that the human world is even more amazing than she imagined. But when Ursula comes ashore disguised as the beautiful Vanessa and puts Eric under a spell, Ariel's many friends must come from "under the sea" to thwart the sea witch and help bring Ariel and Eric together.

MOMENTS TO REMEMBER

- Ariel is late to her performing debut alongside her sisters because she's exploring a sunken ship with Flounder. They encounter a shark and just manage to escape with their lives (and some goodies).

- When Prince Eric's ship catches fire, Ariel rescues the young man and returns him to shore. After making sure he's all right, she swims away before anyone can see her. But Ariel finds she's in love with a prince!

- In a desperate attempt to punish his daughter, King Triton destroys Ariel's secret grotto. Ariel seeks out the sea witch, Ursula, and makes a deal that will give her legs and allow her to live on land so she can meet Prince Eric. The price? Her voice.

- Ursula's plan is to use Ariel to get to King Triton, as she forces the king to yield his power in order to save his daughter. A battle ensues, and Prince Eric saves Ariel—defeating the sea witch forever.

THINGABOBS, GADGETS, AND GIZMOS IN ARIEL'S GROTTO

- Statue of Prince Eric
- Fork
- Pipe
- Candelabra
- Clock
- Globe
- Eyeglasses
- Corkscrews
- Books
- Paintings
- Jack-in-the-box
- Knight's helmet
- Jewelry

- Various chests and trunks
- Pocket watches
- Lanterns
- Coatrack
- Music box
- Vases
- Musical instruments
- Birdcage
- Bottles
- Bell
- Mirrors

CHARACTERS

ARIEL

FLOUNDER

SEBASTIAN

SCUTTLE

KING TRITON

ARIEL'S SISTERS

URSULA

FLOTSAM AND JETSAM

PRINCE ERIC

MAX

GRIMSBY

CARLOTTA

Disney
Beauty and the Beast

BELLE AND MAURICE'S HOUSE

BOOKSELLER

TAVERN

VILLAGE
SQUARE

BEAST'S CASTLE

Disney
Beauty and the Beast

Belle feels stuck in her poor provincial town somewhere in the French countryside. While her village is quite charming with its cobblestone streets, small shops, fountain, and pastoral surroundings, no one there quite understands Belle's dreaming, penchant for reading, and refusal to marry town heartthrob Gaston.

Though she yearns for adventure beyond the constraints of her home, Belle gets more than she bargained for. Just outside her village, beyond a spooky, wolf-filled forest, a mysterious, long-forgotten cursed castle lies waiting for its rescuer. The castle is first Belle's father's prison and then hers, a place filled with enchanted characters, a frightening beast, an air of loneliness, and dark secrets.

In time, Belle's nightmare turns into a dream come true. With the help of a softening Beast and his loyal servants, Belle makes friends, gets the biggest library she's ever seen, and falls in love. Once the castle's residents fight off a threatening mob, everyone (except Gaston) gets a happily ever after.

MOMENTS TO REMEMBER

- The castle and all its residents are cursed when an enchantress casts a powerful spell. She leaves behind an enchanted rose. If the Beast cannot learn to love someone and earn her love in return by the time the last petal falls, the spell will last forever.

- Maurice stumbles upon the Beast's castle after getting lost on his way to an invention fair. When Belle finds him imprisoned in the castle, she immediately offers to take his place.

- Belle runs away from the castle and encounters a vicious pack of wolves in the woods. The Beast saves her life, but is injured in the process. Belle begins to see him as more than just a beast.

- Just as the last rose petal falls, Belle tells the Beast she loves him—breaking the curse and transforming him back into a prince.

EVERYTHING ENCHANTED

- Beast (prince)

- Featherduster (housemaid)

- Teapot (housekeeper)

- Teacup (housekeeper's child)

- Candelabra (maître d')

- Clock (majordomo)

- Wardrobe (lady's maid)

- Ottoman (dog)

- Stove (chef)

- Suits of armor (knights)

- Coatrack (valet)

CHARACTERS

BELLE   THE BEAST   GASTON   LEFOU

MAURICE   PHILIPPE   LUMIERE   COGSWORTH

MRS. POTTS   CHIP   THE FEATHERDUSTER   THE WARDROBE

DISNEP

CAVE OF WONDERS

Aladdin

N

S

SULTAN'S
PALACE

JASMINE'S
GARDEN

MARKETPLACE

ALADDIN'S
HIDEOUT

AGRABAH

Aladdin

Somewhere in the Middle East lies Agrabah, city of "mystery and enchantment." Agrabah is bustling with street performers, livestock, and a bazaar selling everything from rugs to fruit to pottery to fish to jewelry. Rising above the streets are open-windowed apartments offering relief from the hot climate, as well as places for a street rat to hide out while he's on the run from the royal guards.

On the other side of the palace walls, it's a different world entirely. The Sultan's home is a massive display of wealth, with grand rooms, park-sized gardens, and the finest trimmings and furnishings. While the danger of going hungry or being thrown in the dungeons is a threat on the streets of Agrabah, very different dangers lurk in the Sultan's palace in the lair of evil royal vizier Jafar.

Beyond Agrabah and its palace is a desert wasteland filled with miles and miles of sand. It's rumored that somewhere in that desert, hidden by an ancient magic, is a cave of wonders filled with treasure beyond anyone's wildest fantasy.

MOMENTS TO REMEMBER

- Aladdin first meets Jasmine when she's sneaking around the streets of Agrabah in disguise, looking for an adventure outside the palace.

- Persuaded to enter the Cave of Wonders by Jafar, Aladdin and Abu are trapped inside after Abu touches a forbidden treasure. But they manage to keep hold of the old lamp Jafar wanted, which has a genie living inside!

- Aladdin uses his first wish to become a prince and win over Jasmine. "Prince Ali" takes Jasmine on a magic carpet ride, showing her sights like the pyramids of Egypt, statues in Greece, and fireworks in China.

- After defeating Jafar, Aladdin keeps the promise he made to the Genie when they first met. He uses his third wish to set his blue friend free.

PRINCE ALI'S ENTOURAGE

- Sixty elephants
- Seventy-five golden camels
- Drummers riding real camels
- Fifty-three purple peacocks
- Giant gorilla balloon
- Ninety-five white Persian monkeys
- Swordsmen
- Belly dancers
- Forty fakirs

- Jugglers
- Bears
- Lions
- Llamas
- Birds
- Cooks
- Bakers
- Bell ringers
- Flag bearers
- Acrobats
- Brass band

CHARACTERS

ALADDIN

JASMINE

THE GENIE

ABU

THE MAGIC CARPET

THE SULTAN

RAJAH

JAFAR

THE ROYAL GUARDS

IAGO

THE
LION KING

RAFIKI'S
ANCIENT TREE

PRIDE
LANDS

JUNGLE

ELEPHANT
GRAVEYARD

PRIDE ROCK

SCAR'S LAIR

Disney
THE
LION KING

The Pride Lands of Africa are a place where harmony is everything and lions reign supreme. As Mufasa describes to Simba, "everything the light touches" is their kingdom.

The circle of life is key to the stability of the Pride Lands. Birth and death, predator and prey are all natural parts of the cycle that keeps these lands healthy and thriving. Mufasa instructs Simba that every creature is to be respected, "from the crawling ant to the leaping antelope." When the animals die, they become part of the earth, and the circle of life continues.

The tree-spotted, grassy plains of the Pride Lands' savannah offer a place for herds to graze and predators to hunt. Outside the savannah is a desert region marked by sandy dunes and cracked, dry ground. Beyond the desert is a jungle oasis full of lush trees and vegetation, flowing waters, and grubs galore. Simba travels a great distance to flee Pride Rock, and a great distance back to reclaim his throne, restoring the balance so essential to the land.

MOMENTS TO REMEMBER

- All the animals of the Pride Lands travel to Pride Rock in peace and harmony to see and celebrate King Mufasa's new son and heir, baby Simba.

- Simba and Nala are itching to explore a shadowy place beyond the kingdom's borders where they're not supposed to go—the Elephant Graveyard. They run into a band of hyenas, proving Mufasa's warnings to keep away were right.

- After Simba flees the Pride Lands, Timon and Pumbaa teach the young lion their motto: *hakuna matata*. It's a lifestyle with no rules, no responsibilities, and no worries. Simba adapts to this as he grows into an adult in his jungle home.

- Simba returns to the Pride Lands with Nala, and he sees how, under Scar's reign, the environment is overhunted, drought-stricken, and devastated. When Simba defeats Scar and takes back his kingdom, the Pride Lands flourish once again.

PRIDE LANDS TIPS

- BEST LOOKOUT SPOT: Pride Rock is the center of the Pride Lands, and a great place to observe the kingdom.

- BEST POUNCING SPOT: wherever Zazu is, of course!

- BEST PLAYTIME SPOT: water hole (NOT the Elephant Graveyard)

- PHRASE TO LIVE BY: *hakuna matata*

- BEST NIGHTTIME ACTIVITY: Stargazing. To connect with the past, just look to the sky—great kings of the past are always watching from the stars.

- FOR EXOTIC EATING: Let Pumbaa educate your palate with a bug tasting menu in the jungle.

- ROMANTIC GETAWAY: The waterfalls are a breathtaking backdrop for falling in love.

CHARACTERS

SIMBA

NALA

MUFASA

SARABI

RAFIKI

ZAZU

PUMBAA

TIMON

SCAR

SHENZI

BANZAI

ED

Disney · PIXAR

TOY STORY

PIZZA PLANET

DINOCO

VIRTUAL REALTY

JUJU'S HOUSE O' FOOD

Bud's

Tasty Treats

OLD TOWN

TRI-COUNTY EAST SCHOOL

FOR SALE
VIRTUAL REALTY
SOLD

SID'S HOUSE

ANDY'S OLD HOUSE

Disney · PIXAR

TOY STORY

Andy lives on a quiet suburban street in a family-friendly neighborhood. With good schools, parks, and playgrounds, it's a great place to grow up. And the blue-sky walls of Andy's bedroom are the perfect backdrop for his toys. Life is good for Woody and the other toys in this room full of imagination and fun.

Andy plays with his toys often, but when the toys are alone, they climb out of their covered wagon toy box and get to work. They catch a glimpse of the outside world through Andy's bedroom window. Whether it's figuring out how to rescue a friend left outside or watching a visitor pull into the driveway, they're able to keep an eye on everything going on in the neighborhood. Sometimes, they may even jump out of the window to venture into the world.

MOMENTS TO REMEMBER

- Andy is a boy who loves playing with all his toys, but his favorite is Woody, a pull-string cowboy doll. Then he gets an impressive birthday gift: Buzz Lightyear, the latest, greatest space action figure.

- Woody tries to get Buzz out of the way so that Andy will pay attention to him again, but the plan backfires. He finds himself lost in the world outside Andy's room with Buzz as his only companion.

- Trapped inside Sid's house, a disappointed Buzz finally realizes that he's not a real space ranger. And Woody must confront his deepest insecurities to convince Buzz that being a toy is the most wonderful job in the world.

- With help from Sid's mistreated toys, Buzz and Woody finally work together, scaring the daylights out of Sid, racing a moving truck, and soaring through the sky, before at last finding their way back to Andy.

BEST ARCADE GAMES AT PIZZA PLANET

- Scooter Attack
- Whack-a-Alien
- Annihilator
- Kabookey!
- Planet Killer
- Black Hole
- Do Unto Others
- Space Crane
- Combat Wombat
- Rocket Ride

CHARACTERS

ANDY

WOODY

BUZZ LIGHTYEAR

BO PEEP

REX

HAMM

MR. POTATO HEAD

SLINKY DOG

THE ALIENS

SID

SCUD

RC CAR

MUTANT TOYS

DISNEY · PIXAR

a bug's life

↑ THE CITY

DRY RIVERBED

CASEY JR COOKIES

CASEY JR COOKIES

P.T. FLEA'S CIRCUS WAGON

ANT ISLAND

THRONE ROOM
AND COUNCIL
CHAMBER

THE ANTHILL

OFFERING
STONE

BUG BUNKER

INFIRMARY

Disney · PIXAR
a bug's life

Ant Island has a beautiful tree at its center, big boulders at its shore, and an ant community living beneath it all. Twisted tree roots serve as paths connecting the various rooms that make up the ant colony.

When Flik sets off on an adventure to help his friends, he uses a dandelion seed to float off one of the island cliffs. The wind sends him crashing into a boulder in the arid riverbed below, but he dusts himself off and begins his journey into the unknown, determined to return a hero.

MOMENTS TO REMEMBER

- Each and every day, the ants spend the bulk of their time working, walking in lines, and gathering food. And then, each and every season, a gang of grasshoppers led by the sinister Hopper arrive at the ant colony's offering stone and collect all the food.

- The council meeting room is where big dilemmas are discussed, while major decisions—like the one to boot Flik off the island—are made in the courtroom.

- Flik goes to the edge of Ant Island and sails away on a dandelion puff, finally arriving in The City. He is sure he'll find bugs rough enough to stand up to the grasshoppers, and he does: the circus bugs!

- On the day the grasshoppers arrive, the circus bugs and the ants work together to stop Hopper. Their plan to scare him away with a fake bird goes awry, but one way or another, the ant colony will never again have to worry about going hungry.

ANT ISLAND INFO

- GOVERNMENT: Monarchy

- ANTAGONISTS: Grasshoppers

- CURRENCY: Food

- TYPES OF BUGS:
  - Ants
  - Caterpillar
  - Grasshoppers
  - Walking stick
  - Butterfly
  - Ladybug
  - Praying mantis
  - Gypsy moth
  - Black widow spider
  - Pill bugs
  - Rhinoceros beetle

CHARACTERS

DOT

ATTA

FLIK

THE QUEEN

HOPPER

P.T. FLEA

HEIMLICH

FRANCIS

MANNY

GYPSY

DIM

SLIM

TUCK AND ROLL

ROSIE

Disney · PIXAR
FINDING NEMO

A sea anemone in the Great Barrier Reef is the comfortable and cozy home of Marlin and his son, Nemo. With its colorful landscape, good schools, and playgrounds, this section of the reef is a wonderful place to raise a family. But beyond the safety of their home lies the endless ocean, where both adventure and danger lurk, and that's exactly why Marlin believes there is no need to explore foreign waters. EVER.

But when Nemo ventures beyond the reef searching for his independence, he gets caught and ends up inside a dental office fish tank in Sydney, Australia! With the help of newfound friend Dory, Marlin goes on a perilous journey to find his son, encountering the ocean's vast beauty—and threats—while learning to let go.

MOMENTS TO REMEMBER

- On his first day of school, Nemo accepts a dare from his friends and swims out into the open ocean. He unexpectedly gets caught by a diver!

- Marlin asks everyone he can find if they've seen the boat that took his son. Dory says she has and tells Marlin to follow her . . . but Dory has short-term memory loss. Before long, she can't even remember who Marlin is!

- Marlin and Dory run into a group of sharks, are attacked by an anglerfish, get directions from a school of moonfish, end up surrounded by jellyfish, and then catch a ride with sea turtles only to be swallowed up by a huge whale, who helps them get to Sydney Harbour.

- A pelican named Nigel helps Nemo realize his dad is risking everything to save him. With help from the other fish in the tank, Nemo escapes and reunites with his father.

INTRODUCING SYDNEY HARBOUR

- Sydney Harbour is home to some of Australia's big-name attractions, including the Sydney Opera House and Sydney Harbour Bridge.

- The Sydney Harbour Bridge, first opened in 1932, is the world's largest steel arch bridge.

- The East Australian Current is a superhighway that fish and sea turtles use to travel down the east coast of Australia to get to Sydney Harbour.

- Over five hundred species of fish are found in Sydney Harbour.

- At 42 Wallaby Way, visitors will find a dentist's office with an impressive aquarium.

CHARACTERS

MARLIN   DORY   NEMO   CRUSH   SQUIRT

MR. RAY   PEARL   SHELDON   TAD   NIGEL

BRUCE   CHUM   ANCHOR   GILL   JACQUES

GURGLE   PEACH   DEB   BUBBLES   BLOAT

ROCKET LAUNCH TUBE

CONTROL ROOM

KRONOS

METROVILLE

SYNDROME'S BASE

LAVA ROOM

ISLAND OF NOMANISAN

LAGOON

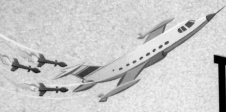

Disney • PIXAR
THE INCREDIBLES

The mysterious island of Nomanisan is the perfect secret lair. On the surface, its lush jungles, waterfalls, and underwater tunnels make it a unique fortress for a villain, but there's even more than meets the eye beyond the walls of cascading lava. It has rocket launchpads, secret passageways, a monorail system, and even robotic birds that stealthily keep an eye on everything.

One of the island's many caves reveals a secret to Mr. Incredible: other Supers have suffered at Syndrome's hands, including his good friend Gazerbeam. Another cave serves as the perfect hiding spot for Dash and Violet as Elastigirl tries to locate Mr. Incredible . . . until the powerful rocket launch sends them running.

MOMENTS TO REMEMBER

- Mirage tells Bob that a top-secret division of the government needs Mr. Incredible's unique abilities. He boards an ultra-sleek jet headed toward the volcanic island of Nomanisan. His assignment: shut down the Omnidroid 9000.

- It isn't long before Mr. Incredible is back on Nomanisan, sporting a new suit and ready to take down another evil droid. This time, the droid's claws tighten around him as Syndrome appears.

- While Elastigirl searches the island for Mr. Incredible, Dash and Violet take on Syndrome's guards. Violet creates a spherical force field around herself and her brother. Dash uses his Super speed inside the force field, and they knock down the bad guys.

- After the family reunites, they fight Syndrome's orbs until Syndrome himself appears! The villain suspends them in midair with his immobi-ray and transports them to a prison chamber. The family soon realizes their strongest Super power is using all their strengths to work as a team.

TECH ON NOMANISAN

- Omnidroid 9000
- Immobi-ray invention
- High-tech security system
- Monorail system
- Robotic bird cameras
- Utility gauntlets
- Miniature explosives
- Rocket boots
- Viper vehicles
- Velocipods
- Manta jet
- Energy prisons

CHARACTERS

HELEN

BOB

VIOLET

DASH

JACK-JACK

KARI

EDNA MODE

FROZONE

MIRAGE

SYNDROME

Disney·PIXAR

Cars

WHEEL
WELL
MOTEL

66

Welcome to
RADIATOR
SPRINGS
Gateway to Ornament Valley

RAMONE'S HOUSE
OF BODY ART

MUNICIPAL
COURTHOUSE &
FIRE STATION

LUIGI'S CASA DELLA TIRES

CADILLAC RANGE

WILLYS BUTTE

N
W E
S

Radiator Springs
Drive-In THEATRE

FLO'S V8 CAFÉ

DRIVE-IN
THEATRE

Radiator Springs
ENTRANCE DRIVE-IN THEATRE

FILLMORE'S
TASTE-IN

SARGE'S
SURPLUS HUT

RADIATOR
SPRINGS

ORNAMENT VALLEY ♦ MECHANICAL CLINIC
DOCTOR HUDSON

ORNAMENT VALLEY MECHANICAL CLINIC

66

COZY CONE MOTEL

COZY
CONE
MOTEL
VACANCY
100%
REFRIGERATED
AIR

TOW MATER
TOWING & SALVAGE

TOW
MATER

RADIATOR
SPRINGS
CURIOS

66
WESTERN
JUNK
FOSSILS

OFFICE

RADIATOR SPRINGS
MUNICIPAL
IMPOUND

66

RADIATOR
SPRINGS CURIOS

Disney · PIXAR

Cars

Welcome to Radiator Springs!

Nestled in the heart of Carburetor County, Radiator Springs is a jewel along the historic Highway 66. Ever since it was founded in the early 1900s, this town has been an oasis in the desert. The residents consider it their job and pleasure to take care of travelers from near and far, whether that means fitting them for new tires, offering them a new paint job, or serving them a good swig of motor oil.

When Lightning McQueen first arrived, he saw Radiator Springs as a boring, sleepy little town struggling to stay on the map. But once he got to know the town and its residents, he grew to love the town enough to make it his home.

MOMENTS TO REMEMBER

- Lightning McQueen first becomes familiar with Radiator Springs when he is sentenced to fix the road he destroyed.

- Before Lightning's big race, he gets new tires, fills up on Fillmore's organic fuel, tries night vision goggles at Sarge's Surplus Hut, picks out a bumper sticker at Lizzie's curio shop, and gets a new paint job at Ramone's House of Body Art.

- Doc Hudson, the town's judge and doctor, is secretly a world-famous Piston Cup racer known as "the Fabulous Hudson Hornet." He teaches Lightning how to race on a dirt track and eventually becomes his crew chief, teaching him that there's more to racing than winning.

- Sally and Lightning explore the outskirts of the small town. Lightning enjoys the stunning view of Ornament Valley, but he's sad that the Interstate encourages cars to avoid Highway 66, steering them away from Radiator Springs. He wants to see Radiator Springs "back on the map," too.

KEY FACTS

- FOUNDED: 1909

- FOUNDER: Stanley

- MAIN ATTRACTIONS: The Hudson Hornet Racing Museum; Willys Butte; Radiator Springs Drive-In Theatre

- LOCAL CUISINE: Flo's V8 Café

- LOCATION: Along Highway 66

- MOUNTAINS: Cadillac Range

CHARACTERS

LIGHTNING MCQUEEN   MATER   SALLY   DOC HUDSON

FLO   RAMONE   LUIGI AND GUIDO   SARGE

FILLMORE   LIZZIE   RED   SHERIFF

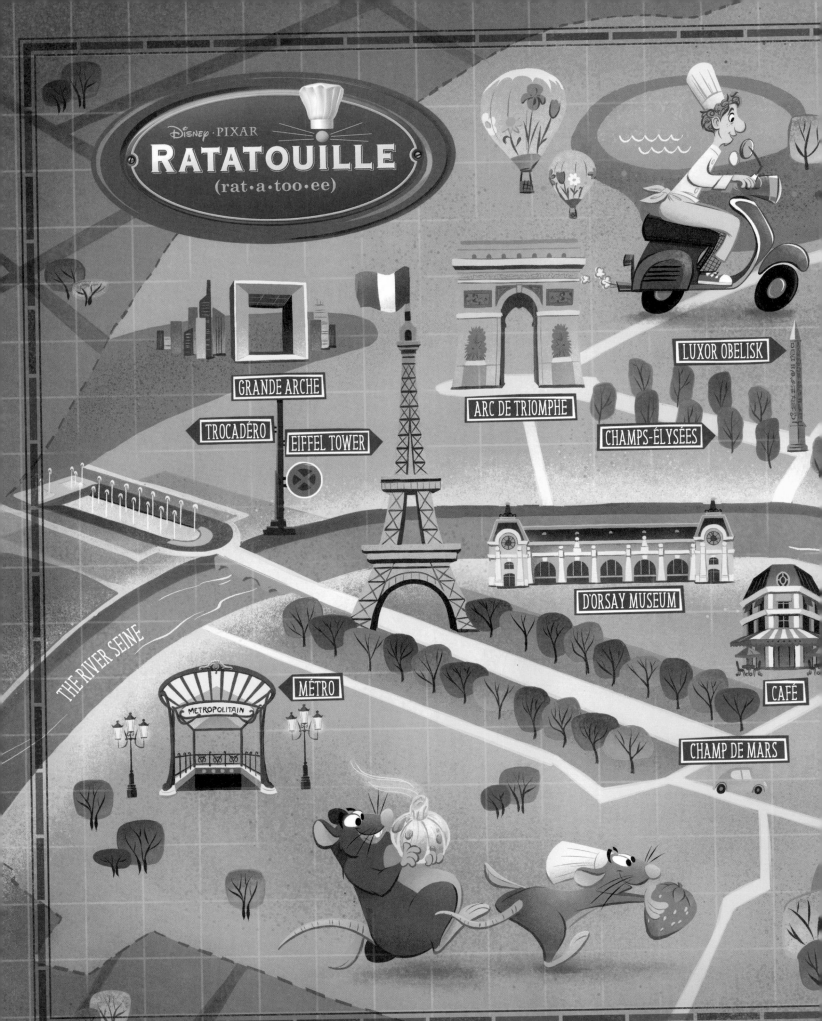

RATATOUILLE
(rat·a·too·ee)

Ahhh, Paris . . . the city of romance and the very best cuisine. Remy the rat is delighted to have finally found a place where people enjoy food as much as he does. When he realizes that Gusteau's, the top restaurant in all of France, has fallen from grace, he discovers his passion as chef and works together with Alfredo Linguini to restore its glory. Eventually, they open the bistro La Ratatouille, offering the very best cuisine to the people (and the rats) of Paris.

MOMENTS TO REMEMBER

- Deep in the French countryside lives a rat colony. One of those rats, Remy, has very big dreams. He wants to be a great chef like his idol, a human chef named Auguste Gusteau.

- The rats live in the attic of an old woman named Mabel. One day, she discovers them and chases them out. All the other rats make it to evacuation boats, but Remy goes back for Gusteau's cookbook. Separated from his family, Remy is swept away to Paris.

- Once in Paris, Remy makes his way to Gusteau's restaurant. He watches in horror as one of the kitchen workers, Linguini, accidentally spills a pot of soup and begins adding ingredients at random. This is Remy's big chance. He can fix the soup!

- The duo realize that Remy can guide Linguini by tugging his hair. Before long, Linguini is chopping, mixing, and pouring—all while blindfolded!

REMY'S LATEST DISHES

- Cheese paired with grapes and a baguette
- Crepes
- Croque monsieur
- Foie gras
- Ratatouille
- Soupe à l'oignon
- Bouillabaisse
- Tomates farcies
- Meringue pie
- Soufflé

CHARACTERS

REMY

EMILE

LINGUINI

COLETTE

GUSTEAU

ANTON EGO

SKINNER

MABEL

Disney · PIXAR

UP

SPIRIT OF ADVENTURE

Spirit of Adventure

PARADISE
FALLS

MUNTZ'S
LAIR

CANYON

N
W E
S

LANDING

CARL'S HOUSE

ROCK
GARDEN

JUNGLE

Disney · PIXAR

After the passing of his wife, Carl decides he wants to leave everything behind. He ties balloons to his house and sets sail for the skies! Unbeknownst to him, a Wilderness Explorer named Russell is on his front porch when he takes off. Carl and Russell's journey across the sky in an old house is not easy—they even have to survive a terrible thunderstorm on their way—but eventually, they do reach their destination deep in South America at the fantastical Paradise Falls. From its lush jungles, strange rock formations, towering mountain peaks, and mysterious caves, the diverse landscape of this region is the perfect setting for adventure.

MOMENTS TO REMEMBER

- After Carl's wife, Ellie, passes away, a real estate developer wants to buy their house, but Carl refuses to sell it. Instead, Carl charts a course to Paradise Falls, South America . . . and brings his house with him, thanks to thousands of balloons.

- When Russell and Carl first arrive after their perilous journey, they tether themselves to the floating house and "walk" it across the unique terrain. Along the way, they meet a lovable talking dog named Dug and a giant bird Russell names Kevin.

- Carl and Russell eventually stop inside a cave that turns out to be the home of the famous explorer Charles F. Muntz, Carl's childhood hero. Carl is shocked to find that his famous *Spirit of Adventure* airship is there, and even more surprised to learn that Muntz is anything but heroic.

- After a fierce battle in the sky atop Muntz's airship, they manage to save Kevin from the explorer's clutches and return home in time for Russell's Wilderness Explorer ceremony.

RUSSELL'S WILDERNESS EXPLORER BADGES

- Ellie Badge
- Hiking
- Bigfoot
- Navigation
- Cell Phone
- Swimming
- Boating
- Fishing
- Insectology
- Zoology
- Gardening
- Weather
- Kite Flying
- Master of Disguise

- Archery
- Karate
- Wild Animal Defensive Arts
- Knot Tying
- Sewing
- Cooking
- First Aid
- Second Aid
- Recycling
- Reading
- Music
- Art
- Badge Overload
- Assisting the Elderly

CHARACTERS

CARL

ELLIE

RUSSELL

DUG

KEVIN

CHARLES F. MUNTZ

ALPHA

BETA

GAMMA

BRAVE

Disney · PIXAR

HIGHLANDS

FIRE FALLS

← WITCH'S COTTAGE

ROYAL DAIS

CABER TOSS AR

CLAN TENTS

CASTLE
DUNBROCH

KEEP

STABLE

MERCHANT AREA

DUNBROCH
KINGDOM

DUNBROCH
HARBOR

Disney · PIXAR
BRAVE

The kingdom of DunBroch in the stunning Scottish Highlands is home to four proud clans: DunBroch, MacGuffin, Macintosh, and Dingwall. Castle DunBroch's many rooms serve King Fergus, his royal family, and their guests quite well, particularly the Great Hall, which is wonderful for dinners, speeches, and the occasional brawl. As in most castles, the kitchen is one of the busiest rooms. Not only is the staff always cooking, they also have to try to keep the triplets from stealing sweets, especially sweets that may turn them into bears!

Just outside is the castle green, a beautiful place for outdoor events including family picnics and the traditional Highland Games. When the allied clans come to DunBroch to compete for Merida's hand in marriage, Merida chooses archery as the sport and seizes her own destiny.

MOMENTS TO REMEMBER

- The royal family welcomes the allied clans in the castle's Great Hall. The heads of each clan step forward to present their sons. Each of the firstborn will compete to marry Merida.

- When Merida fires her own arrows at her suitors' targets, Queen Elinor is furious. But Merida is angry, too, and slashes the family tapestry between the images of her and her mother, then flees from the castle on her horse, Angus.

- Merida follows the will-o'-the-wisps into the forest to a small cottage. There, she meets a witch who gives her a spell to change her mum. Merida doesn't realize the spell will change her mother into a bear!

- To reverse the spell, Merida thinks she has to find the family tapestry and mend it. But nothing happens until Merida tells her mother "I love you."

TRADITIONAL HIGHLAND GAMES

- Archery
- Caber toss
- Haggis flip
- Stone put
- Hammer throw
- Cake toss
- Tug-of-war

CHARACTERS

MERIDA

QUEEN ELINOR

KING FERGUS

HARRIS, HUBERT, AND HAMISH

MAUDIE

ANGUS

MOR'DU

THE WITCH

LORD AND YOUNG MACINTOSH

LORD AND YOUNG MACGUFFIN

LORD AND WEE DINGWALL

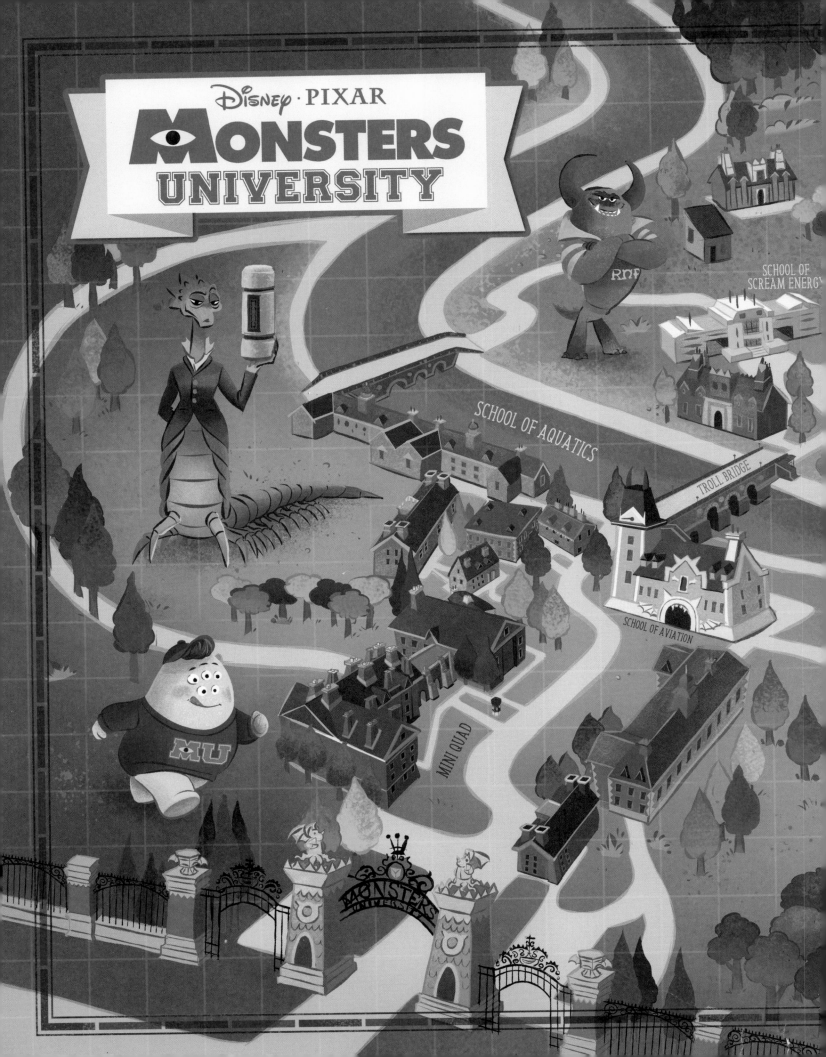

Disney · PIXAR
MONSTERS UNIVERSITY

Monsters University, founded in 1313 by Arthur Clawson, isn't the kind of school you end up at by accident. Ask any student, and they're likely to tell you they've been dreaming of attending MU since they were a larva, grub, egg, puggle, or chick.

The campus offers a wide variety of majors, from canister design to door building, but the most prestigious and competitive program at Monsters University is, without doubt, the School of Scaring.

Located on the outskirts of Monstropolis, MU is far from the hustle and bustle of city life, providing creatures big and small with an ideal setting for learning, playing, and socializing—just don't upset the librarian.

With its beautiful buildings, landscaping, cobblestone walks, and an actual troll under the bridge, every student is bound to have an unforgettable college experience at MU.

MOMENTS TO REMEMBER

- Mike Wazowski and James P. "Sulley" Sullivan meet in Scaring 101 . . . and do not get along. During their final exam, they get into a huge fight and are both kicked out of the School of Scaring!

- Mike and Sulley make a deal with Dean Hardscrabble. If their team wins the Scare Games, she'll let them all into the Scare Program. If they lose, they have to leave MU for good. Their team is a fraternity called Oozma Kappa. Its members are not scary . . . at all.

- Soon the Scare Games begin! Mike and Sulley quickly realized that if they work as a team, they can win. There's more than one way to be scary. Finally only two teams are left—the RORs and the OKs. The last event? SCARING!

- And they win! But because Mike and Sulley break the rules and go into the human world, they are expelled from MU. They decide to be mailroom workers at Monsters, Inc. Together, there's nothing they can't do.

MU FUN FACTS

- KNOWN FOR: Top School of Scaring

- FAMOUS GRADUATE: "Frightening" Frank McCay

- RIVAL: Fear Tech

- SCARE GAMES FOUNDER: Dean Hardscrabble

- SCARE GAME ACTIVITIES:
  - Toxicity Challenge
  - Avoid the Parent
  - Don't Scare the Teen
  - Hide and Sneak
  - Simulated Scare

CHARACTERS

MIKE WAZOWSKI

JAMES P. "SULLEY" SULLIVAN

RANDY BOGGS

DEAN HARDSCRABBLE

DON CARLTON

SCOTT "SQUISHY" SQUIBBLES

ART

TERRI AND TERRY PERRY

JOHNNY WORTHINGTON

PYTHON NU KAPPAS

MS. SQUIBBLES

ARCHIE THE SCARE PIG

Disney

FROZEN

FJORD

THE SOUTHERN ISLES

ARENDELLE
CASTLE

W N S E

ARENDELLE

VALLEY OF THE
LIVING ROCK

ELSA'S ICE PALACE

THE NORTH
MOUNTAIN

WANDERING OAKEN'S
TRADING POST AND SAUNA

Disney FROZEN

Don't let the cold weather scare you away, for in the kingdom of Arendelle, the winter holds magic in its ice and snow. Accessible by land or by fjord, Arendelle is a lovely place to visit in the summer months, but the snowy peaks are where it really holds its charm.

When the castle gates are open, the villagers outside can mix and mingle in the courtyard. There's plenty to do and see in the village, from the busy docks to the market.

In the mountains beyond the castle and village lie even more intriguing places, such as the Valley of the Living Rock and the North Mountain, which is home to an ice palace guarded by an intimidating snow monster. A smaller, friendlier snowman named Olaf was born nearby, so if he's around, it's good to be aware that he likes warm hugs.

MOMENTS TO REMEMBER

- When Anna and Elsa are girls, Elsa accidentally strikes Anna with her magic, knocking her unconscious. The family travels to the trolls for help. Grand Pabbie saves Anna by removing all her memories of magic. Elsa must now hide her gift.

- When it's time for Elsa's coronation, the sisters host members of the neighboring kingdoms for the first time in forever. Elsa accidentally reveals her magic and goes into hiding, freezing the kingdom as she flees.

- Anna, Kristoff, Sven, and Olaf track Elsa to the North Mountain, where she's created an ice palace. Elsa asks her sister to leave, and in a burst of emotion, she accidentally strikes Anna with her magic once again.

- Anna's heart begins to freeze from the magical blow. Moments before she freezes solid, Anna shields Elsa from a deadly attack. This act of true love saves them both, and Elsa frees Arendelle from its winter spell.

SUMMER SALE AT OAKEN'S

- Family sauna packages
- Carrots
- Shovels
- Pickaxes
- Rope
- Floral arrangements
- Snowshoes—winter stock, only a few left!
- Snow boots—almost gone!
- Bathing suits
- Clogs
- Sun balm—Oaken's own recipe!
- Bread

- Fruit
- Wood-carved bear and troll figurines
- Aloe vera
- Variety of sleeveless dresses

CHARACTERS

ANNA

ELSA

KING AGNARR

QUEEN IDUNA

KRISTOFF

SVEN

OLAF

PRINCE HANS

THE DUKE OF WESELTON

BULDA

GRAND PABBIE

OAKEN

MARSHMALLOW

Disney · PIXAR

INSIDE OUT

FAMILY ISLAND

HONESTY ISLAND

HEADQUARTERS

HOCKEY ISLAND

FRIENDSHIP ISLAND

GOOFBALL ISLAND

TRAIN OF THOUGHT

DREAM
PRODUCTIONS

SUBCONSCIOUS

IMAGINATION
LAND

ABSTRACT THOUGHT

LONG TERM MEMORY

Disney · PIXAR

INSIDE OUT

Riley's mind is a vast, busy place, and at the center of it all are her Emotions: Joy, Sadness, Anger, Fear, and Disgust. Each Emotion has an important purpose, taking his or her turn at the control panel—or console—and guiding Riley through everyday tasks, interactions, and challenges.

Inside Headquarters, gears whir and spin, sending Riley's memory spheres rolling along rails as they are directed and organized on shelves—until the end of the day, when they are sent out to the mazelike Long Term Memory.

Beyond Headquarters lies the seemingly endless and changing Mind World with the Islands of Personality, Imagination Land, Abstract Thought, Dream Productions, the Subconscious, Long Term Memory, and the Train of Thought running through it all.

MOMENTS TO REMEMBER

- As Riley struggles to adjust to her new life in San Francisco, tensions among the Emotions escalate inside Headquarters. Joy and Sadness compete for control, and both are knocked into the far reaches of the Mind World.

- Determined to find their way back, as Riley now needs help, Joy, Sadness, and Bing Bong explore unfamiliar parts of the mind. Along the way, Joy learns that Riley needs Sadness to feel happy again.

- Riley's five Islands of Personality—Family, Honesty, Hockey, Friendship, and Goofball—are powered by Riley's core memories, the important memories that come from big moments in her life. After Riley turns twelve, new islands emerge, such as Boy Band Island.

- Bing Bong is Riley's old imaginary friend! He is part cat, part elephant, and part dolphin, and is made of cotton candy. He and Riley had many adventures in his song-powered wagon rocket.

INSIDE IMAGINATION LAND

- French Fry Forest

- Trophy Town

- Cloud Town

- Lava!

- House of Cards

- Imaginary Boyfriend Generator

- Preschool World
  - Graham Cracker Castle
  - Sparkle Pony Mountain
  - Princess Dream World
  - Stuffed Animal Hall of Fame

CHARACTERS

RILEY

JOY

SADNESS

ANGER

FEAR

DISGUST

BING BONG

JANGLES

THE FORGETTERS

RAINBOW UNICORN

TE FITI

LALOTAI

TAMATOA'S LAIR

MAUI'S ISLAND

Moana lives in the middle of a vast ocean, the promise of adventure waiting just beyond the reef—but she's never left the shores of Motunui, her island home. A thriving, self-sufficient island, Motunui is Moana's future—at least, that's what she's told. With its peaceful, happy people, plenty of fish, the ever-useful coconut, and tropical beauty everywhere you look, who could want more?

But Moana knows her destiny is at sea, not on land; just like her ancestors, she is a voyager at heart, meant to explore. When she sets sail to find Maui and restore the heart of Te Fiti to save her dying island, she gets her chance. The water is a universe of its own, with Kakamora roaming the seas, a lurking underworld of monsters, a demigod in hiding, Te Kā raging, and Te Fiti dying. When she finishes her journey, Moana is ready to use her new sailing and wayfinding skills to lead her people back to the open waters.

MOMENTS TO REMEMBER

- When Moana is a toddler, she wanders to the beach, drawn to the water. The ocean "chooses" her, giving her the heart of Te Fiti.

- Gramma Tala shows Moana a cavern that holds a stash of boats that belonged to her ancestors. Tala urges Moana to take the heart of Te Fiti and find Maui in order to save Motunui.

- When Moana meets Maui, he steals Moana's boat and traps her in a cavern. With some ingenuity and help from the ocean, Moana gets her boat back, and the two learn to work together.

- Moana almost gives up after Maui deserts her and she's nearly bested by Te Kā. But Gramma Tala appears in spirit form and tells Moana to look inside herself and summon the strength to save her island.

MAUI'S ACHIEVEMENTS

- Used his magical fishhook to shape-shift

- Pulled up the sky

- Stole fire from down below

- Lassoed the sun to make days longer

- Harnessed the breeze so ships would sail and trees would shake

- Pulled islands up from the sea

- Buried an eel's guts to sprout coconut trees

- Battled Tamatoa and ripped off one of his legs

- Stole Te Fiti's heart to give to the humans

You're welcome!

CHARACTERS

MOANA   MAUI   GRAMMA TALA   CHIEF TUI

SINA   HEIHEI   PUA   TE FITI

KAKAMORA   TAMATOA   TE KĀ

COCO

Disney · PIXAR

MARIACHI
PLAZA

SANTA CECILIA CEMETERY

N

W   E

S

TOMB OF ERNESTO
DE LA CRUZ

OFRENDA ROOM

MIGUEL'S ATTIC

RIVERA COMPOUND

RIVERA

SHOE STORE

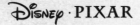

Disney · PIXAR
COCO

Santa Cecilia is a colorful little village in the heart of México. With its lively shops, open markets, and warm residents, it's easy to see that this is home to many families who value their culture, history, and ancestors. On any given day, the village is alive with music and decorated with papel picado.

Miguel was born here, and he lives in a home with his large family, the Riveras. The Rivera family is well known for their shoemaking, and they have one family rule: No music! But Miguel has a secret—he loves music.

In the plaza in the center of town stands a statue honoring Ernesto de la Cruz, the greatest musician of all time (according to Miguel).

MOMENTS TO REMEMBER

- During Día de los Muertos, Abuelita breaks Miguel's guitar. Miguel runs through the streets of Santa Cecilia to the tomb of Ernesto de la Cruz. Believing the famous musician is his great-great-grandfather, Miguel borrows the guitar from the tomb. But something goes wrong. No one can see him!

- Together with his ancestors and his dog, Dante, Miguel goes across the glowing Marigold Bridge that connects the Land of the Living and the Land of the Dead.

- In the Land of the Dead, Miguel meets Héctor. Héctor offers to help Miguel find his great-great-grandfather if Miguel takes Héctor's picture back with him to the Land of the Living.

- When it's time for Miguel to go home, he promises Héctor that he'll be remembered. Miguel plays a song for Mamá Coco, a song Héctor used to sing to her when she was little. Slowly, her face brightens as her memories of him flood in.

OFRENDA TRADITIONS

- The word *ofrenda* means "offering" in Spanish.

- Ofrendas are set up so families can remember and honor the memory of their ancestors.

- Every ofrenda includes the four elements: water, wind, earth, and fire.

- For each deceased relative, a candle is lit.

- The cempasúchil, a type of marigold flower native to México, is often placed on ofrendas.

CHARACTERS

MIGUEL

DANTE

ERNESTO DE LA CRUZ

HÉCTOR

MAMÁ IMELDA

PEPITA

MAMÁ COCO

ABUELITA

MAMÁ

PAPÁ

And they lived . . .

HAPPILY EVER AFTER

. . . well, most of them!

ACKNOWLEDGMENTS

Special thanks to Tessa Roehl and Suzanne Francis for writing the text for this book, and a special thanks to Caroline LaVelle Egan for her hard work gathering the reference for the maps, as well as for her stunning map artwork. An additional special thanks to Nick Balian, Scott Tilley, and the Disney Storybook Art team for helping with the map artwork. Finally, a special thanks to Meg Roth for her work as an editor on this book.